DETECTIVE DINOSAUR

DETECTIVE # 823
M. Dinosaur

by James Skofield
pictures by R.W. Alley

Sandy Creek

*For Sara Lamb, who gave
me my first book about dinosaurs*
—J.S.

*For Mary and Lynn, keepers of the
Children's Room at the Barrington
Public Library*
—R.W.A.

Detective Dinosaur
Text copyright © 1996 by James Skofield
Illustrations copyright © 1996 by R. W. Alley

This 2010 edition licensed for publication by Sandy Creek
by arrangement with HarperCollins Publishers.

Sandy Creek
387 Park Avenue South
New York, NY 10016

ISBN-13: 978-0-7607-8150-0
Manufactured in China.
Manufactured 04/2012
Lot 12 13 SCP 10

Contents

Dinosaurs in the story

Tyrannosaurus	(tih-ran-uh-SAW-russ)
Diplodocus	(dip-LAH-duh-cuss)
Pterodactyl	(ter-eh-DAK-tul)
Stegosaurus	(steg-uh-SAW-russ)

"Drat!" said Detective Dinosaur.

"Where is my hat?

It is missing."

Detective Dinosaur looked

in his desk.

No hat.

He looked on his bookshelf.

He looked in his wastebasket.

He saw a banana peel

but no hat.

Brrrrrring! The phone rang.

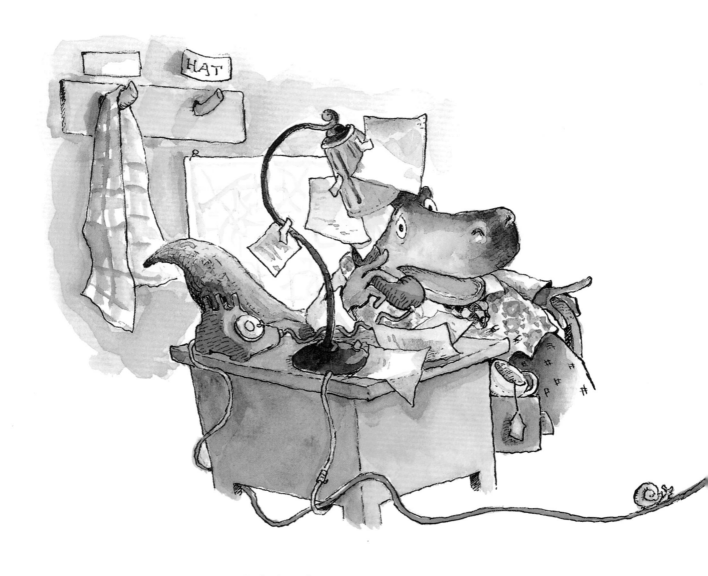

It was Chief Tyrannosaurus.

"Chief," said Detective Dinosaur,
"something awful has happened!
My hat is missing!"

8

"That is awful,"

said Chief Tyrannosaurus.

"Ask Deputy Diplodocus

at the Office of Missing Hats.

Maybe he has seen your hat."

"Okay, Chief," said Detective Dinosaur.

9

He went to the Office of Missing Hats.

He saw big hats and small hats,

silk hats and straw hats.

"Where is my hat?"

he asked Deputy Diplodocus.

"It is still missing!"

"I am sorry," said Deputy Diplodocus.

Detective Dinosaur walked away

and ran into Officer Pterodactyl.

"You look sad, sir," she said.

"I have just come

from the Office of Missing Hats,"

said Detective Dinosaur.

"I saw many hats,

but I did not see my hat.

Drat! It is still missing!"

"But, sir," said Officer Pterodactyl,

"what is on your head?"

Detective Dinosaur reached up.

He felt something on his head.

"It is my hat!"

cried Detective Dinosaur.

"It is no longer missing!

Officer, how can I ever thank you?"

"No need, sir,"

said Officer Pterodactyl.

"Glad to help out."

The Case of the Squeaking Shoe

Detective Dinosaur

and Officer Pterodactyl

were on patrol one morning.

Squeak!

Each time Detective Dinosaur

took a step,

he heard *squeak!*

17

"Officer Pterodactyl,"
said Detective Dinosaur,
"each time I take a step,
my shoe squeaks!"

"Perhaps it is too tight, sir,"
said Officer Pterodactyl.
"No," said Detective Dinosaur,
"it fits me fine."

"Perhaps your shoe is old, sir,"

said Officer Pterodactyl.

"No, no," said Detective Dinosaur,

"it is brand-new!"

"Perhaps your shoe needs polish, sir,"

said Officer Pterodactyl.

"No, no, NO!"

said Detective Dinosaur.

"I polished it this morning!"

"Then I do not know, sir,"

said Officer Pterodactyl.

21

"I think my shoe squeaks,"

said Detective Dinosaur,

"because it is angry."

"Shoes do not get angry, sir,"

said Officer Pterodactyl.

"Well, mine does,"

said Detective Dinosaur.

"When I was a little dinosaur
and I got angry,

my mother would sing to me.

Now I will sing to my shoe."

Detective Dinosaur sang:

"Oh shoe, my shoe,

do not feel bad.

I am not mean.

I am not mad.

What makes you squeak

with all your might?

Are your shoelaces tied too tight?"

"Oh, go away!" said a small voice.

25

"Did you speak, shoe?"

asked Detective Dinosaur.

"No," said the voice, "I did."

A mouse climbed out of the shoe.

26

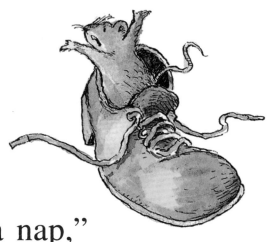

"I was trying to take a nap,"

said the mouse,

"but each time you took a step,

your big foot squeezed me!

Now, let me down and stop singing!'

Detective Dinosaur let the mouse

jump out and run away.

Then he put on his shoe

and took a step.

There was no squeak.

"Hooray!" said Detective Dinosaur.

"My shoe is no longer angry!"

Officer Pterodactyl
shook her head and flew away.
Detective Dinosaur walked on
without a sound.

CASE
CLOSED

Detective Dinosaur

and Officer Pterodactyl

were on night patrol.

It was quiet and dark.

"Psssst! Officer Pterodactyl!"

said Detective Dinosaur.

"I think someone is following us."

"Do not worry, sir,"

said Officer Pterodactyl.

"It is only our shadows."

Suddenly, they heard a noise.

Clang!

It came from down a dark alley.

Detective Dinosaur

and Officer Pterodactyl

tiptoed down the alley.

They peeked around a corner.

They saw a huge dark shadow.

The shadow was slamming

something big and round

on the ground.

CLAAANNNGGG!

Detective Dinosaur

and Officer Pterodactyl

were afraid.

"What is it?" asked Detective Dinosaur.

"I do not know, sir,"

said Officer Pterodactyl,

"but it is big."

"Perhaps it is a robber!"

said Detective Dinosaur.

"But robbers are quiet, sir,"

said Officer Pterodactyl.

"Perhaps it is a monster!"

said Detective Dinosaur.

"Perhaps we should call the Police!"

"We are the Police, sir!"

said Officer Pterodactyl.

"Oh, you are right, Officer,"

said Detective Dinosaur.

"It is up to us!

This is the Police!"

he yelled bravely.

"Come out with your hands up!"

"Thank goodness!" said a little voice.

"Come help me quickly!"

Detective Dinosaur

and Officer Pterodactyl

went around the corner.

They found a little stegosaurus.

42

"My mama told me
to take out the garbage," she said.
"But my tail got caught on this lid,
and I cannot get free!"
The little stegosaurus swung her tail
and slammed the lid on the ground.
CLAAAAANNNNNGGGGG!

"Hold still, little one,"

said Officer Pterodactyl.

She freed the tail.

"Thank you so much!"

said the little stegosaurus.

"Now you better run inside,"

said Detective Dinosaur.

"You do not want your mama

to worry."

Detective Dinosaur

and Officer Pterodactyl

walked back down the alley.

"I am so glad it was not a monster!"

said Detective Dinosaur.

"Do not worry, sir,"

said Officer Pterodactyl.

"I will always protect you."

"Yes," said Detective Dinosaur,

"you are brave, Officer!"

"So are you, sir,"

said Officer Pterodactyl.

Together, the two brave friends
and their shadows
walked on into the night.